Fancy Nancy's Favorite FANCY WORDS

From Accessories to Zany

Written by Jane O'Connor

Illustrated by Robin Preiss Glasser

HarperCollins Publishers

Fancy Nancy's Favorite Fancy Words
Text copyright © 2008 by Jane O'Connor
Illustrations copyright © 2006, 2007, 2008 by Robin Preiss Glasser

Printed in the U.S.A.

Library of Congress Cataloging-in-Publication Data is available.
ISBN 978-0-06-154923-6 (trade bdg.)

Typography by Jeanne L. Hogle
8 9 10

❖
First Edition

In memory of Ole Risom, a wonderful mentor
and great friend, from a grateful wordsmith
—J. O'C.

For my children, Sasha and Benjamin,
who have my heart
—R. P. G.

Bonjour, everybody!

I think fancy words are almost like magic. You can take a plain word like feather and—presto change-o!—turn it into something special . . . a plume!

Fancy words also sound *beautiful* and are fun to say, especially ones in French! (Bonjour means hello.)

So here is a compendium (that's fancy for collection) of my *absolutely* favorite fancy words just for you.

When you use one in a sentence, it's like adding sprinkles to vanilla ice cream!

Love,
Nancy

Accessories—fancy extra stuff

Guess who has more accessories than anybody in the entire world?

Boa—a long scarf of feathers

Boas are very glamorous, but they itch!

Canine—anything to do with dogs

Watch! Frenchy is performing one of her many canine tricks!

Dapper—fancy, for a man

Usually my dad doesn't look this dapper.

Excursion—a special trip

Mrs. DeVine and Jewel make a weekly
excursion to the beauty salon.

Fiasco —a big flop, a disaster

I dropped all the parfaits. What a fiasco!

Gorgeous—even more beautiful than beautiful

Glamorous—stylish and beautiful, like a movie star

I can't decide which of these fancy words I like better, so I included them both.

Hostess—the girl having a party

Bree says I'm a wonderful hostess.
There are always plenty of cookies at my parties!

I am in bed because I am feeling ill
(that's fancy for sick).

Christmas Tinsel

Magic4Kids

Improvise—to use whatever is handy in order to make something

I wanted a canopy bed, so I had to improvise.
I used a sheet, a mop, and a broom!

Joyous—happy

Christmas is a very joyous time of year for my family.

Knack—a talent or a clever way of doing something

Lavender—fancy for light purple

I have a knack for mixing and matching ensembles.
Take it from me, lavender works with almost anything.

Monogram—your initials on something to show it's yours

I wish I had a middle name.
Then my monogram would have three letters.

Nestle—to snuggle and be cozy

Here I am all nestled in bed.

Ooh la la!—French for "Look! How wonderful!"

Ooh la la! I love Mrs. DeVine's glamorous parasol!

Parasol—an old-fashioned umbrella that protects you from the sun

Queen—a woman who rules over a kingdom

Queen isn't really a fancy word, but I love it anyway because it's royal.
(Monarch is a fancy word for king or queen.)

Répondez s'il vous plaît

—fancy and French for "please answer."

Bree's
Butterfly
Birthday

Saturday
at noon

Come
as your
favorite
Butterfly

R.S.V.P.

On invitations, you shorten
it to R.S.V.P.

Souvenir—something that reminds you of a special place

See the gorgeous souvenirs I got on vacation.

Tiara—a crown for a princess

A princess is supposed to keep her tiara on!

Understated—plain

My mother wears such understated clothes.

Vocabulary—all the words you know

After you read this book, your vocabulary will be gigantic!
(That's fancy for really big.)

Wardrobe—a collection of clothes

I have quite an extensive wardrobe.

Xenophile (zen-o-file)

—a person who loves foreign people and foreign things

I am a xenophile. I especially love anything that's French!

Yearn—to want really badly

I yearn to visit Paris someday.

Zany —very silly

Some people might think Jewel looks zany in this outfit.
But I think she's exquisite. Have you ever
seen a dog with more accessories?

Look at all the fancy words you know now!

Accessories
Boa
Canine
Dapper
Excursion
Fiasco

Gorgeous
Glamorous
Hostess
Improvise
Joyous

Knack
Lavender
Monogram
Nestle
Ooh la la!
Parasol
Queen

Répondez
S'il vous
Plaît
Souvenir
Tiara
Understated

Vocabulary
Wardrobe
Xenophile
Yearn
Zany